THE LONG-LOST SECRET DIARY OF THE WORLD'S WORST OLYMPIC ATHLETE

Book design by David Salariya
Illustrations by Isobel Lundie

Published in the United States by Jolly Fish Press, an imprint of North Star Editions, Inc.

First US Edition
First US Printing, 2020

Library of Congress Cataloging-in-Publication Data (pending)
978-1-63163-446-8 (paperback)
978-1-63163-445-1 (hardcover)

Jolly Fish Press
North Star Editions, Inc.
2297 Waters Drive
Mendota Heights, MN 55120
www.jollyfishpress.com

Printed in the United States of America

THE LONG-LOST SECRET DIARY OF THE WORLD'S WORST OLYMPIC ATHLETE

Written by
Tim Collins

Illustrated by
Isobel Lundie

JOLLY
FiSH
PRESS

Mendota Heights, Minnesota

Chapter I

⊢—⊣

Athens,
380 BC

Welcome to my life!

Day I

Welcome to this record of all my amazing victories! Athens is the greatest city in the world, and I, Alexander, am its strongest hero! Even the mighty Heracles would run away and cry if he saw me.

I shall detail all my achievements, which include:

- *Strangling snakes*
- *Wrestling lions*
- *Capturing mad bulls*
- *Punching giant crabs*

Well . . . er . . . actually, I've not really done any of these things yet. But I did accidentally startle a cat once. I suppose it was more of a kitten to be honest.

I just wanted to start my scroll like that in case Dad reads it. He says I'll only become a true hero if I convince myself that I'm cut out to be one.

But sometimes—and I'm sure he'll never read this far, so it's okay to write it—I wonder if I really am.

8

Dad is tall and strong and has a face scarred from years of war. I'm small and thin, with a face that falls into a natural look of fear.

But that's just for now. I'm going to change. I know because an oracle said so.

Your son is destined for great things . . . honest!

Years ago, Dad spoke to a wise woman in a temple. She told him he'd have a son who would win a great victory in the field of battle and be cheered by huge crowds.

Two years later, I arrived. Mom and Dad don't have any other children, so the oracle must have been talking about me.

I haven't done anything very amazing yet, but I've spent most of my life at home, and it's not easy to be a great hero without going anywhere. It's not like three-headed hellhounds just turn up at your house. You have to go and find them.

So I've asked Dad to send me off to fight in a war. I'm sure my heroic side will kick in when I'm in actual danger.

GET REAL

An oracle was a priest or priestess who
could pass on messages from a god. Many
people believed these messages revealed
what would happen in the future. The
most famous oracle was the oracle of
Delphi, who was said to communicate
with the god Apollo.

Day 2

I had a great idea this morning. I decided to put on Dad's armor and announce to him that I was ready for war.

I went up to the bedroom and grabbed his breastplate, leg guards, helmet, spear, and shield. I probably should have waited until I got down, because it was quite hard to use the stairs with all that stuff on.

II

It didn't help that Dad was sitting in the courtyard and watching me the whole time. I'd wanted to make a dramatic entrance and pledge to fight for the glory of Athens, but the impact was lessened as he stared at me hobbling downstairs.

I didn't expect all that stuff to be so heavy. Soldiers march from dawn until dusk with it all on, which must be really tough.

I was so out of breath by the time I reached the bottom of the stairs that I had to repeat my big announcement a few times before Dad could understand it.

Instead of agreeing and rushing off to arrange things, Dad went into a long speech about his army days.

12

I really wanted to sit down because the armor was so heavy, but I thought it would be more heroic to keep standing up straight.

As Dad went on and on, I felt my shoulders drooping and my knees buckling. Just as Dad was in the middle of a big description of a glorious battle, I found myself keeling forward and clattering to the floor.

Crash!

Dad leaped up and yelled at me. He said that if I couldn't even listen to a story about the army without fainting, I had no chance of actually fighting in it. I tried to explain that it was just the armor that had made me fall over, but he just stomped away.

Day 3

Dad wasn't around today, so I spent all morning telling Mom about what a great hero I'm going to be. I moved my stool around so I could talk to her while she was making bread, spinning cloth, and mending Dad's tunic. I don't think she really understood, because she kept nodding and saying, "That's nice, dear." Nice? I was talking about how I was going to defeat some man-eating birds with beaks made from bronze. She should have been terrified.

What's the most heroic way to stand on a stool?

After a while, she stared into the distance for a moment and then asked if I'd be gone for a long time if Dad let me fight in the army.

I said I would.

Mom smiled for the first time all day and said she'd talk to Dad about it. I'm surprised she'd be prepared to go for ages without seeing her beloved son. Maybe my heroic tales have inspired her to make a sacrifice herself.

GET REAL

*Women didn't have much freedom in
ancient Greece. They were usually under
the control of their fathers or husbands
and would spend most of their time in
the home. But this wasn't true in every
city. For example, women in Sparta were
allowed education and property.*

Day 4

Today, I had another great idea to turn myself
into a hero. I decided to make a sacrifice to the
gods. That's the way to make things happen.

I couldn't find any animals to sacrifice, so I
decided to use one of Mom's pots instead.

I dragged it over to the altar in our courtyard and smashed it with a stick while asking Athena to make me wise and strong.

Mom, Dad, and all of our slaves rushed out to see what I was doing. Before I could explain, Dad grabbed the stick and sent me upstairs.

Sometimes I wonder if they really want me to become a hero.

GET REAL

The ancient Greeks worshipped many different gods and goddesses, each of whom looked after different aspects of life and death. Athena was associated with warfare, courage, and wisdom.

Day 5

My sacrifice has worked! Athena must have listened, because I'm about to leave my life as a housebound loser behind and become a hero.

Dad went out to speak to some of his friends this morning. When he returned, he announced that I would be accompanying one of them, called Dracon, on an important mission.

I kept asking Dad who we were going off to fight, but he wouldn't tell me anything until Dracon arrived.

I grabbed my stick and practiced battling while I was waiting. Unfortunately, I got a little carried away and accidentally hit Mom as she was rushing out of the kitchen. In my excited state, I thought she was a barbarian trying to ambush me.

Dad broke my stick in two, and I had to sit quietly in the courtyard and wait for Dracon.

Snap!

Finally, he arrived. But he didn't look like what I was expecting. Instead of wearing armor and carrying a sword and shield, Dracon wore just a short, thin tunic. He was as strong and tall as you'd expect a great soldier to be, but he didn't have many scars. And his skin was smooth and glistening, like he'd rubbed oil into it.

He swept his hands through his short blond hair and planted his hands on his hips. He asked if I was the young boy who was going to help him with the games.

I was about to say I didn't know anything about any games, but I was ready to fight in a war, when Dad jumped in and said I'd be overjoyed to accompany him to Olympia.

Dracon told me all about the games, but I didn't really take it in. At first I was so disappointed that I wasn't going to get to attack anyone with a spear that I couldn't concentrate.

But then Dad gave me a talk about how dangerous it would be and I got interested. He said we'd have to travel far through hostile lands to get to Olympia. He then said Dracon would be competing in the pentathlon against the strongest and fittest men from every city, and if he won, it would bring glory to Athens. Dracon would be a great hero, and I'd be one too for helping him.

I paced around the courtyard, imagining the adoring crowds. I decided it was a pretty good idea after all.

GET REAL

The first Olympic Games were held in 776 BCE, according to a record of winners. They were held every four years after that and lasted for five days. The pentathlon featured five events: the sprint, javelin, discus, long jump, and wrestling.

Chapter 2

Journey to Olympia

Day 6

Dracon arrived outside our house early this morning on a large white horse, whose name was Aethon. There were lots of sacks balanced over Aethon's back.

I was a little disappointed that we didn't each get a horse, as I thought this would be more fitting for a pair of amazing heroes. But I didn't want to start our quest on a bad note, so I asked Dracon to help me on the horse.

Dracon said Aethon was already carrying enough weight, and as the assistant on the journey, I was expected to follow on foot.

I was going to point out that I'm small and I don't weigh much, but I didn't think this would make me sound like good hero material. Plus, Dad says that when you're in the army, you

have to walk long distances all the time, so I
didn't argue.

I said goodbye to Mom and Dad and promised
to return as a great hero. Mom was probably
crying, though the murky light of the early
morning made it look more like she was
breathing a sigh of relief.

We made our way down the hill toward the city
wall as the sun was rising. I looked at the last
houses and a little voice in my mind asked if
it was really such a good idea to leave Athens
behind. It was the best place in the world, and
everywhere else was bound to be disappointing.

I told this voice to shut up. Leaving home and
going on a quest is a vital part of being a hero.
We wouldn't be telling stories about Odysseus
if he'd only made it down to the market for
some figs.

Outside the wall, we followed long tracks through farms where workers were picking olives and loading carts.

I tried to go as fast as I could, but Dracon kept having to stop Aethon to wait for me.

27

We went on and on until the sun began to set ahead of us. Dracon jumped down from Aethon, sat on a large rock, and took a swig from his waterskin.

I tried to sit next to him, but my legs were so wobbly, I found myself flopping forward and curling up on the ground.

I asked Dracon if he could put the tent up without my help, and he burst out laughing.

He pointed to the large mountain ahead of us and said our day's journey wouldn't be over until we were well on the other side of it. Apparently, we were only stopping for our evening snack.

I felt my bottom lip quivering, but I forced myself not to cry. I pulled myself onto the rock, took a swig of water, and bolted down my chunk of bread. Then I forced myself up and started up the mountain path on my aching feet. I told Dracon he could catch up when he'd had enough rest.

We were over the top of the mountain and halfway down the other side by the time Dracon said we could set up camp for the night. Our tent turned out to be nothing but a few animal skins draped over some sticks, but I don't really care. After all that walking, I'd sleep even if we had no shelter and Zeus himself was prodding me with lightning bolts.

My legs are so numb I can hardly feel them. But I don't mind. I'm sure I'll go through much worse on the path to becoming a true hero.

GET REAL

Odysseus was the hero of Homer's epic poem The Odyssey, *written around the eighth century BCE. It describes his ten-year journey home after the Trojan War and the strange creatures he meets, such as sirens, nymphs, and a cyclops. It is still read today and is considered to be one of the greatest stories of all time.*

Day 7

I was woken up by Dracon shaking my shoulders and telling me we needed to get moving. I passed the message on to my legs, but they ignored it.

I got Dracon to pull me up, and I tried to walk. Pain shot up my legs with every step.

I told myself the agony would go away if I ignored it. And the first part of our route was downhill, so it seemed manageable.

Dracon loaded the animal skins into the sacks on Aethon's back and got going. I limped after him.

Aethon was going slowly down the rocky path, which meant I finally had a chance to talk to Dracon as we traveled.

I asked him how long it would be until we got to Olympia. We'd already traveled so far that I'd assumed a couple more days would do it. So when Dracon said we could make it in just nine days if we kept up the pace, I felt myself panic.

My pulse sped up, my mouth went dry, and the path ahead of me swam back and forth. My legs buckled, and something big and flat smacked me in the face. It was the ground.

When I came to, I noticed to my surprise that I seemed to be moving. Then I noticed to my even greater surprise that I had somehow become incredibly tall too.

I looked around and realized I must have fainted. Dracon had put me on Aethon and was walking ahead of us.

This wasn't good. I'd only come along to help him, and I was already making things more difficult.

Day 8

I feel bad about being on Aethon. What if Dracon wears his legs out so much he can't compete in the Olympics?

Sorry to be a burden.

I'm too ashamed to speak to Dracon, but I find
that Aethon is a good listener. I've got this
weird idea that he can understand what I'm
saying. I know it can't be true, but it's helping
to pass the time anyway.

Day 9

When we were stopping for a break today, Dracon asked me how long I'd been riding horses. He was shocked when I said it was my first try.

He patted Aethon on the forehead and told him he'd been good to accept a new rider so well, and I realized I'd done well too.

In my first few days of riding, I haven't fallen off Aethon or made him panic and bolt. I haven't even struggled to get on or off him. In fact, it's all been so easy I hadn't considered that it could be any other way.

Heroes like riding horses. I like riding horses. This is good.

Day 10

We went past some mean-looking locals with scraggy beards and dirty faces today. I offered to guard Dracon and Aethon if they tried to attack.

Dracon said I wouldn't need to, as anyone on the way to or from the games is considered a pilgrim and under the protection of the gods. Even if there was a huge battle going on, the fighters would stop to let us through before going back to chopping one another's heads off.

So it sounds as though Dad was exaggerating the dangers of our route to get me excited. Not that I'm complaining. Those locals looked very nasty to me.

GET REAL

Traveling in ancient Greece could be dangerous. Greece was made up of many different city-states that were often at war with one another. But if you were on the way to Olympia for the games, you were protected by a sacred truce. Anyone attacking you would risk angering the gods.

Day 16

Dracon says we should be in Olympia by tomorrow. It's over the range of hills just ahead of us. There are a few other athletes, as well as some market traders and officials, on the same track as us now. Some are on foot, while others are riding carts dragged by mules.

Dracon says many more will arrive when the games themselves start. Those who can't come overland will arrive by sea on cramped ships.

I asked Dracon why they held the games somewhere so far out of the way. He said there are plenty of games held in places that are easier to reach, but the gods chose the ones in Olympia to be the best. If you really want to feel like a champion, you have to win there, however long it takes to reach.

GET REAL

The Olympic Games were just one of four major athletic competitions in ancient Greece. The others were the Pythian Games, the Nemean Games, and the Isthmian Games. Despite being the hardest to get to, the Olympic Games were regarded as the greatest, and superstar athletes would list their Olympic victories first.

37

Chapter 3

Life in Olympia

Day 17

We're finally here. Olympia is actually very impressive, and I can see why the gods like it so much. It's set in a wide plain surrounded by green hills. A wide river with small streams breaking off it runs through the middle.

We found a good place for our shelter near the river, and the other athletes and visitors have taken spots nearby. It already seems very busy, but Dracon says that when the fans arrive, it's going to be ten times as crowded. The whole plain, right up to the hills, will be filled with people, some sleeping on the ground and others staying in large tents attended by armies of slaves.

Right now, it seems impossible that such a huge amount of people could descend on such a secluded place, like an entire city will sprout legs and wander across the land.

Day 18

We had more of a chance to explore today, and I still think Olympia is pretty astonishing. Obviously, I'm from the greatest city in the world, so I'm used to seeing brilliant things, but it's still quite a shock to see them in the middle of nowhere. And if I think they're good, imagine what someone from an inferior city will think.

There's the stadium, which is a long track between two sloping stands for spectators. It has thin starting and finishing lines made of stone and a patch of rough ground for the long jump.

Near that is the hippodrome, where the horseback and chariot races will take place. This has a longer track and bigger stands, as well as the stables where we've housed Aethon with the other horses.

Farther on from that is the council house, where Dracon has to register for the games.

But the most impressive area of all is called the sanctuary, which is full of sacred things like altars and statues. The best part is the Temple of Zeus. This is a huge stone building with thick pillars, colorful sculptures at the top, and a tiled marble ceiling. Inside is an absolutely massive statue of Zeus made of ivory and gold.

Gazing up at his huge beardy face helps you realize how serious these games actually are. We're not just here to prove Athens is the best city in the world, even though we will. We're also here to honor the king of the gods.

GET REAL

The statue of Zeus at Olympia was about 43 feet (13 m) tall. It was created by the sculptor Phidias in the fifth century BCE and was destroyed in the fifth century CE. It was one of the seven wonders of the ancient world, along with the Colossus of Rhodes, the Hanging Gardens of Babylon, the Mausoleum at Halicarnassus, the Temple of Artemis, the Lighthouse of Alexandria, and the Great Pyramid of Giza, which is the only one to have survived.

Day 19

My tasks as Dracon's assistant have been quite straightforward so far. While he's training, I have to fetch him water and make sure he has his oil flask, sponge, and scraper. Then I have to buy him figs, olives, fish, and bread from the stalls in time for his food breaks.

This last task is harder than the others because I have to haggle. I've never bought food before, and it takes a bit of getting used to.

For example, I went out to buy some bread today. The man at the stall, who has a fixed scowl, wanted four obols, and I was about to count them out from Dracon's purse when I heard a loud argument going on at the next stall.

Give me your dough!

45

I stopped to listen. The vendor wanted two obols for the bread, but the customer only wanted to pay half an obol. After a long and intense discussion, which involved the customer pretending to walk away three times, they finally agreed on one obol.

This made me realize I should be paying the same amount. But just like the other customer, I had to argue for ages. At one point, I thought the man was about to stone me to death with some of his staler loaves, but he eventually gave in.

A new customer approached the stall, and the whole thing started again.

Meanwhile, I walked back to our shelter with my throat aching and my forehead throbbing. Haggling is so exhausting they should include it in the pentathlon.

46

GET REAL

Athletes in ancient Greece would compete naked and covered in oil. The oil helped to protect their skin from the sun, and the act of rubbing it in might have helped prepare their muscles for exercise too. Wrestlers added a layer of dust to the oil so they could get a grip on each other.

Day 20

Dracon was practicing his sprint on the stadium track this morning, and it was making him so thirsty I had to keep going off to refill his waterskin.

The river wasn't far, but I saw some of the other athletes using it as a toilet and thought the water might have an unpleasant aftertaste. So I trekked up to a stream flowing down from one of the mountains, which no one had relieved themselves in. The only problem was that Dracon was so thirsty every time I returned that he'd gulp down the water and send me straight back.

After my tenth trip, I saw that a man with curly hair and a thick black beard was practicing alongside him. The man pointed at me and asked Dracon how much I'd cost. I didn't understand what he meant until he added that his own servant had cost just ten drachmas and could move twice as fast.

How much for your puny servant?

48

I tried to keep myself calm while I corrected the fool. I told him that I was Dracon's special assistant, not his servant, and that I was a vital part of the team who would also be crowned a hero when Dracon won.

The man said that Dracon wasn't going to win the pentathlon, but if he did, the glory would be for him alone, not his water-carrier.

I tried to ignore him, but it did seem sort of convincing. After all, when you hear people talking about the great athletes of the past, they never mention who their assistants were. And there are no team games in the Olympics. It's all about individual glory. I wondered if Dad might have been exaggerating when he said I'd be a great hero too, just like he exaggerated about the journey being dangerous.

After the man had gone, Dracon told me that he was called Ariston, and he would also be competing in the pentathlon. Ariston comes from Sparta, where everyone is boastful and rude, so I should take no notice. He just wants to annoy us, as he thinks it will give him the edge in the competition.

Day 21

Dracon was practicing javelin today, and I helped him by fetching it from wherever it landed. It feels like quite a heroic event, because javelins are also used to kill enemies in war. They aren't quite the same kind, though. The military ones have sharp iron blades designed to cut through the flesh of enemies. These ones are lighter, with bronze ends that are only meant to leave a mark in the ground. But it would still give you quite a headache if one smacked you between the eyes.

50

Dracon is really good at it. He wraps a small piece of leather around the middle of the javelin and winds it around his fingers. Then he runs up to the starting line and slings it ahead. The javelin flies through the air, rising and dipping in a long arc. Dracon can throw it so far along the track that fetching it made for another exhausting day.

Ariston turned up to practice too. He kept chuckling to himself and timing his throws so they almost hit me.

Dracon told me not to worry, as Ariston was just teasing and would never actually throw the javelin directly at me. This would count as a violent act in a sacred site, and it would anger the gods. I considered throwing myself into the path of the javelin to make the gods think he'd done it on purpose. But I guessed that the gods would probably know what really happened. You can't fool them.

It doesn't matter anyway, because Ariston will get all the punishment he deserves when Dracon beats him.

When Dracon was done, he let me have a go. I tried to do just like he did, wrapping the leather around my fingers, running up to the line, and

52

releasing the javelin. It shot away to my left, briefly flying high, then plummeting down into the exact place on the stand where the judges would be sitting.

I heard horrible laughter and turned to see Ariston bent double and wiping the tears from his eyes. Come on, it wasn't that funny.

GET REAL

Ancient Greek athletes tied a small leather strap around the middle of the javelin. They would create a loop and place their first and middle fingers into it before starting their runs and letting go. The strap made the javelin go farther, and it also helped with accuracy. It was important to leave a mark in the ground that the judges could measure.

Day 22

Dracon trained with the discus today. The discus is a round slab of bronze that you have to throw from the starting line. It's a bit like the javelin event, except that you don't run up. You have to twist around as you throw so that the disc spins through the air and goes really far.

Dracon does it amazingly fast and sends the disc flying far down the track. He made it look incredibly easy, but then some other athletes turned up to practice, and they weren't anywhere near as good.

The more I see Dracon compete, the more convinced I become that he'll win. I've seen a lot of very strong and very fit athletes around here, but he's the greatest by far.

I have no doubt he'll win the laurel wreath and we'll return to Athens in glory.

When we do, I might not mention my own efforts, though. Dracon let me try this event too when he was finished. I stood on the starting line and rehearsed the spinning movement he does. When I thought I'd gotten the hang of it, I spun around as fast as I could and let go of the discus, hoping it would fly through the air.

Unfortunately, I tripped on my own leg while I was doing it, and the discus flopped straight down to the ground, rolled along a little, and then stopped.

Dracon was so embarrassed he pretended to have been too busy scraping his oil off to see how I'd done.

Day 23

One of the jobs I have to do every day is go to the stables and check on Aethon. I find I can tell him things I wouldn't admit to Dracon, like how I wish I was better at the events. I sometimes wonder if I should stay awake all night and practice with the javelin and discus until I can do them properly.

But what would be the point? I'm here to help Dracon, not to take part myself. If I can carry his food, water, oil, and scraper; fetch his javelin and discus; and generally make things easier for him, I'll have made a contribution to his victory, and I'll have plenty to feel proud about.

Day 24

Dracon moved on to the long jump today. This involves leaping along the patch of ground in front of where the judges sit. You need special weights for it, which are curved pieces of bronze or stone that you hold in each hand. Dracon has brought his own weights from home.

He runs up to the line and jumps into the air, holding the weights out. After a while, he throws his arms back and drops the weights. It's amazing how far along this gets him. For a few moments, it's like he's riding along on an invisible horse.

Unlike the javelin and discus, the long jump
didn't seem to involve any complicated twisting
or spinning. I was convinced that if he let me
use his special weights, I could make a good
attempt at it.

This time, I didn't even wait for Dracon to offer.
As soon as he finished practicing, I grabbed
his weights and raced along to the starting

line. I thought about how impressed he'd be when he saw me flying through the air on my first attempt.

Unfortunately, the long jump wasn't as easy as Dracon makes it look.

I jumped and tried to throw my arms out, but the weights were so heavy they swung down

59

again straightaway. They dragged me back,
and I thumped to the ground on the wrong side
of the starting line. I'd managed to jump a foot
in the wrong direction, worse than should have
been possible.

I got back to my feet and gave Dracon's weights
back to him, pretending that I'd just been
checking them rather than actually attempting
a long jump. As we walked out of the stadium, I
noticed Ariston again.

He was with some others this time. There
was a young boy of about my age and height,
and a bald man with a red beard. This time,
they weren't laughing. They were pointing at
me and having a serious conversation, which
was somehow worse, like I was so bad it
had stopped being funny and become
fascinating instead.

GET REAL

Each competitor in the ancient pentathlon had their own special jumping weights, which were called halteres. They were made of stone or metal, and were designed to make the athletes jump farther. Athletes would thrust them forward while taking off, then swing them back and drop them before landing.

Day 25

Today, I was given a very important duty. Dracon was practicing the final event of the pentathlon, which is wrestling, and I had to be his opponent.

Dracon explained the rules to me as we covered ourselves in dust. You need to throw the other person to the ground by grabbing him above the waist or tripping his feet. You have to move around in a circle before lunging forward and grabbing his arm, side, or neck. Then you shove him to the ground, and if he touches it with his hip or back, it counts as a fall. You win if your opponent falls three times.

Dracon said his actual opponents will be much bigger and heavier than me, and that he'd seriously hurt me if he wrestled me for real, but that I could still help him practice his grabs and his footwork.

62

We got started. Dracon hopped about with his arms out and his head down. I did the same, waiting for the moment to lunge forward and grab his arms. I knew I was only helping him practice, but I thought about how much he'd respect me if I really managed to throw him.

I decided to surprise Dracon by going for his shoulders. But just as I was about to, I felt my knees bend and found myself crashing down. At first, I thought Dracon had tripped me, but then I realized I'd fallen over my own legs.

I got back up and tried again. This time, I tried grabbing Dracon's neck, but he leaped aside, sending me flat on my face.

I tried again, this time spinning around to grab the side of his body. But I ended up collapsing in a heap as he jumped back.

And that was it. I'd fallen three times and Dracon had won. This must have been a first in the history of wrestling. Dracon had managed to win without actually touching me.

We both agreed that it might be less distracting for him to practice with an imaginary opponent instead.

Chapter 4

The Spartans

Day 26

Dracon went back to the sprint today. At one point in the morning, a thin man with a long nose came over and asked Dracon about his training. The man rubbed his chin and examined Dracon as they spoke. After a while, he nodded and walked off.

I couldn't work out what he was up to, but Dracon explained that the man is a gambler. He's trying to work out who is most likely to win each event so he can bet on them. Most people just back athletes from their home city, so you can make money if you stay neutral and do your research.

Gambling is forbidden, but Dracon says you can't really stop it. People are so convinced their cities will win that they'll stake all the coins they can find on it.

Day 27

I was putting Aethon back in the stables this afternoon when I noticed the young boy I'd seen with the Spartans. He was just as small and thin as me, and I couldn't help wondering if he was going through the same thing.

It's not easy to admit you're bad at sports when you're surrounded by all the muscle-bound giants of Olympia. I thought I might finally have found someone to share my disappointment with who wasn't a horse.

I went up to the boy and asked him if he was Ariston's assistant. He looked as if I'd just smacked him in the face with a particularly heavy discus.

He crossed his arms and said of course he wasn't an assistant. He was Charilaus, the greatest horse rider in Sparta. And as Sparta was the greatest city in the world, that made him the greatest rider in the world.

I asked him if he wasn't a little short to be a brilliant athlete.

I'm the best.

He sighed and said he'd been told Athenians were stupid, but no one had prepared him for exactly how dense they are. He said that a horse wouldn't be able to go fast if it had a heavy man on it. The best jockeys were always small boys.

That did make a lot of sense. It also explained why Aethon took so well to me.

I told the boy he might be a great rider, but he was just as horrible as all the other Spartans.

Jeez, sorry I asked!

GET REAL

The horseback race in the ancient Olympics needed a different type of athlete. Instead of tall, strong men, the riders would be light young boys. But they would also need to be highly skilled. With just reins to hold on to, staying on the horse for the furious race up and down the hippodrome track was tough. Those who fell off could get trampled by the other horses, risking injury or even death.

Day 28

Dracon was back on sprint practice today. When he was taking a fig break, I asked him why the Spartans are so horrible. They're Greeks and not barbarians, yet they're as uncouth as people from the far ends of the earth. It doesn't seem right.

Dracon explained that the Spartans have always done things differently. Sparta is organized more like an army than a city. All the boys are raised to be soldiers and are deliberately treated badly so they grow up tougher.

They raise their girls to be just as fearsome, as they think a child will be healthier if it comes from two fit parents.

The result is a bunch of people with the strength of Athenians, but none of the wisdom that sets us apart from animals.

Knowing all this stuff about the Spartans only makes me look forward to Dracon's victory even more. I can't wait to see the looks on the faces of the Spartan fans.

GET REAL

One of the reasons it's hard to speak generally about ancient Greece is because the Spartans did things very differently. They valued military power above all else and discouraged anything artistic. It was a city of fighters, not poets, philosophers, or scientists.

The Night Before the Games Begin

The games start tomorrow, and Olympia has been steadily filling up for the last few days. When we first arrived a few weeks ago, I imagined what this place would be like when it was full. I didn't get anywhere close to what it's really like.

73

There are now thousands of tents. Some are just scraps of cloth propped up on sticks, but others are huge structures housing rich men and their many slaves.

You can barely see the tents through the haze of dust that's constantly kicked up by the visitors. The whole village is noisy and smelly, full of rotting food and flies.

The river has now been transformed into a huge toilet. I saw someone bathing in it this morning. They came out dirtier than when they went in.

The stream at the bottom of the mountain still seems clean, luckily, as no one can be bothered walking that far to pee. So at least I can still find fresh water for Dracon.

All around us, people are telling stories about Achilles and Odysseus, arguing over who will win, and comparing war scars.

I can't sleep, but luckily Dracon can, and that's the important thing. He started snoring straight after lying down tonight, and I hope he can keep doing this right up until his event on the third day.

It might even give him an advantage if the other competitors are kept awake by all the noise.

Day One of the Olympics

This is it. The games are underway. We had the opening ceremony today, where all the athletes and judges had to go to the sanctuary and swear their oaths.

A huge crowd gathered around an altar. Two strong men carried a wild boar over. I had to look away while a priest stabbed his knife into it to sacrifice it to Zeus.

He cut the dead boar up and gave pieces to the athletes, who swore to abide by the rules. Then he gave bits to the judges, who promised to be fair and not to take bribes.

After that, the athletes took tokens out of an urn to sort out who would face who in the fighting events. Dracon drew Ariston in the wrestling part of the pentathlon. Ariston let a smug grin spread over his face, though I have no idea why, because Dracon will definitely beat him easily.

I thought Ariston might yell out some insults, but he kept quiet. The whole ceremony was very solemn, in fact. The atmosphere was respectful and religious rather than rowdy and competitive. But that all changed when the events got underway.

We had only a few today, and they were just the ones for young boys, which are meant to prepare us for the proper ones. But even these packed out the stadium with visitors from every city yelling about how they were the best.

I was allowed to watch from near the front with Dracon. We were just behind the row of judges, who all had purple robes, and who were grasping wooden rods for punishing rule-breakers.

The first event was the sprint. A group of about twenty boys lined up along the starting line. They all seemed to be around my age, or maybe younger, though they were all much taller and stronger.

They all got into the same position, with their left feet on the front of the line and their right feet behind it.

A judge looked carefully up and down the line
to check they were all in the correct position.
Then he shouted, "Go!"

The thousands of spectators all began to shout at once, and I made the mistake of looking around at them instead of watching the racers. By the time I had my eyes back on the track, the race was over.

The judge had declared a boy from Corinth to be the winner, which was causing a clump of fans on the other stand to celebrate wildly.

Two of the boys had collided halfway along the track and were clutching their legs and screaming on the ground. A massive argument was flaring up between two rival sets of supporters behind us, which must have been about whose fault this was.

I was watching them shove each other and wondered if they were going to start rioting, but they soon calmed down to watch the next event, which also happened to be a fight.

It was the same event I'd practiced with Dracon. Well, not exactly the same. Nobody lost without their opponent touching them, for example.

The pairs of young fighters were very well matched, and they tended to circle each other for a long time before making their first grabs.

This might sound boring, but the tension of waiting to see who would strike first was actually quite gripping. The winners of each bout had to fight each other until there was just one pair remaining. They were a tall boy from Sparta and a boy from Thebes who looked like a bear. I supported him, just so the Spartans didn't get an early win.

And he did win, though he was so exhausted by the time he'd got through all the bouts that he couldn't even celebrate.

Another fighting event was next: boxing. This one was so gruesome it was hard to watch. All the fighters wound leather straps around their wrists before taking part. I'm guessing these were to protect their hands, but they also cut the faces of their opponents as they smashed into them. I'd rather have sore hands and a face that isn't gushing blood.

Each match went on until one of the fighters surrendered by holding a finger up, by which time they both looked like they'd been savaged by a three-headed hellhound. And, like the wrestlers, the winners of each fight went on to another one, opening deeper wounds.

The crowd loved it, but I had to watch through my fingers. I know I want to be a great military hero one day, and I shouldn't be scared of violence, but it's pretty horrible when you actually see it.

82

GET REAL

Fighting events were incredibly popular at the ancient Olympics. There were contests in wrestling, boxing, and pankration, a brutal variation of wrestling. The city-states of ancient Greece were almost constantly at war, and the ability to inflict and suffer pain was greatly respected.

The First Night

There was no point in trying to sleep tonight. The crowd was even louder than last night, and when I heard a man right next to our shelter announce he was going to tell the entire story of Odysseus, starting with the end of the Trojan War, I realized I might as well get up and explore.

I wandered toward the food stalls, and it wasn't long before I was stuck in a big crowd. Hundreds of men were addressing the masses that were huddled around them. Some were reciting the great tales of the gods and heroes, just as you would expect. But there were more unusual topics too.

A man with a deep voice was telling the story of a sea battle which the Corinthians had recently won, to loud cheering.

Three poets were reading out victory odes about winners from previous years. They were standing next to one another and trying to outdo one another with their descriptions of the strong bodies and noble characters of their subjects. When they'd finished, they all outlined how much they charge for an ode and asked us to recommend them to the winners over the next few days.

A man with a gray beard was drawing a smaller crowd by talking about some patterns he'd noticed in the stars. Some of the movements he was talking about took years, so it's not surprising that he had to wait until he was so old to tell everyone about them.

The strangest speakers of all were two philosophers who were having a huge argument. It was hard to follow exactly what they were talking about, but it had something to do with whether things were real or not. I gave up trying to understand it after a while. I've already got enough to worry about without questioning what exists and what doesn't.

The crowd liked it, though. People were cheering and jeering the opposing thinkers as though they were watching a wrestling match. I left them to it.

The effort of trying to understand the philosophers finally tipped me over into exhaustion. I staggered back to our shelter and collapsed into a deep sleep.

I've just woken up. It's shortly after dawn, and most people still seem to be awake. Are they really going to stay up for the whole five days? Or will they burn out too soon and miss all the good events?

GET REAL

As well as sports, visitors to the Olympics could be entertained by poets, actors, war heroes, scientists, and philosophers. With tens of thousands of visitors around, it was easy to gather a crowd. If you wanted to become famous in ancient Greece, the Olympics was a great place to start.

The Second Day of the Olympics

We were all back in the stadium this morning
for the fighting events. The ones for boys were
bad enough, but the adult ones were even
more brutal.

Wrestling was first. Huge, scar-covered men
lined up to face one another. The judges
patrolled around as the men fought, tapping
the men with their rods and reminding them
of the rules. It was hard to know which fight to
watch, as the sounds of falling and screaming
drew my eye to different bouts. Fighters were
eliminated in each round, until finally a huge
man called Lykos of Argos was declared
the winner.

A huge cheer rang out. Dracon explained that Lykos had won the contest in the last two Olympics, and tales of his strength had been spreading ever since. It's said he can pull trees out of the ground with his bare hands and snap them in two over his knee. It must be a great advantage when people are saying things like that about you. All you have to do is show up and your opponents will be terrified.

Boxing was next, and it was even bloodier than the boys' event. The boxers ran out into the stadium, all displaying the evidence of their previous battles. Their noses had been broken and were set at strange angles, their ears were huge and swollen, and their faces were lined from years of hard punches.

The men could strike with more power than the boys, gouging deeper cuts, which spurted blood all over the ground. It soon looked like everyone had been sacrificing animals to Zeus rather than taking part in a sporting event.

The rule of continuing until a fighter raised their hand in submission still applied, but some boxers kept going until they couldn't even do that, and the judges had to drag them off, leaving a trail of blood.

The winner was a man from Thebes called Milon. He smiled as the judges declared him the victor. Two loose teeth fell out of his mouth as he did so.

But neither of these events were as horrifying as the one that came next. It was called pankration, and it's a sort of cross between wrestling and boxing without as many rules. According to Dracon, the only things you aren't allowed to do are bite someone or gouge their eyes out, but other things that are just as painful are allowed.

The fighters were kicking, punching, twisting, crushing, pulling, and generally trying to snap one another in two.

As with the other fights, it's over when someone surrenders, or passes out, or dies.

But pankration is all about showing how much pain you can take. One fighter got stuck in a hold while his opponent pulled his neck back to stop his breathing. His face went blue, and it looked like he would have to surrender, but he somehow managed to wriggle free and get his opponent into a hold instead. The crowd loved it.

Dracon says that if you surrender before you've suffered enough, you'll bring shame to your city and everyone will despise you when you return. No wonder they're all so proud of their scars.

I don't know how those pankration fighters put up with so much pain. I roll around on the courtyard ground and scream if I catch my foot on our altar. How are you meant to keep going with broken toes?

Watching something like the pankration makes me wonder if I'm really cut out to fight in a war after all. Even if I grew really tall and strong, it wouldn't make pain any less painful. I'd be faced with enemies even more barbaric than a Spartan, and there would be no judges to stop it all if I held my finger up.

But it doesn't really matter what I want. The oracle said I'd end up winning a great battle, so it's going to happen. I just hope I don't get too many limbs pulled off along the way.

I looked away from the battles, but the grunts, cries, and snaps were enough for me to know what was going on. By the time of the final, Dracon nudged me and told me I was missing a brilliant fight. I glanced down to see a huge man from Sparta leaning over another huge man from Syracuse, who was lying flat on the ground. The Spartan was pummeling the Syracusan in the face, and I wondered if he'd killed him.

I could see the Spartan fans on the opposite stand cheering and holding their arms in the air. They thought the victory was theirs.

But in a final burst of energy, the Syracusan jumped to his feet and hooked his arm around the Spartan's neck. He thumped his fist against the Spartan's skull over and over until the Spartan had no choice but to surrender.

The judges declared the Syracusan the winner, and the bloody, dusty, sweaty fighter threw his hand into the air. I noticed that two of his fingers were now sticking out at odd angles.

It was sickening to watch, but at least I got to enjoy the disappointment on the faces of the Spartan fans.

After that, I went to get Dracon his evening bread and figs. The food stalls get busier every time I go, and it takes me longer to get back through the crowds.

I'm writing this while Dracon is eating his figs. He's offered me some, but I don't feel hungry because I'm still thinking about that horrible pankration match.

The running events are next. The short sprint is so important that the entire Olympics will be named after the winner. Everyone was frantically placing bets on it as I made my way back just then.

GET REAL

The pankration was the most popular of the fighting events at the ancient Olympics. It was also the most violent, with everything except biting and eye-gouging permitted. And even those might be attempted if a judge was looking away. Some competitors would suffer broken bones, and some even died. Arrhichion of Phigalia was said to have both died and won. He was dying of strangulation when his opponent surrendered, and the judges had no choice but to declare the dead fighter the winner.

Chapter 5

Fall of a Hero

The Afternoon of the Second Day

Every bit of space on and around the seating stands was rammed with spectators for the running events.

Fans were even lining the slopes of the mountain far behind us. They'd no doubt traveled for days to get here, only to see nothing but tiny dots in the distance when it came to the main event. But at least they'd be able to tell their friends back home that they had been at the Olympics.

First up was the long-distance run, where the athletes had to do twenty laps. The trumpet blasted, and the herald yelled the names and cities of the runners. The biggest cheers were for our Athenian runner Megakles and Lykinos from Sparta.

Lykinos got out in front early, and I was worried that Megakles might fall so far back he'd never be able to catch up. But Dracon told me he was holding his energy back. Running might seem very simple, but you need tactics just like in any other sport.

This turned out to be right. Megakles raced away from the pack on the final lap, but a runner called Sotades from Ephesos did the same thing.

They both overtook the Spartan, but Sotades got in front by a foot and won the race.

The supporters from Ephesos ran down the slope behind us and pushed forward to congratulate their hero.

I told Dracon I was upset that we didn't win,

but didn't really mind, because he was certain to win the pentathlon tomorrow.

He told me it was up to the gods, not him, and he didn't want to anger them by taking his victory for granted. I can see why he would say this, but I still think he'll win. He's so much better than those other losers.

After the celebrating fans had been herded back onto the stand, it was time for the short sprint.

Having missed the boys' version, I was determined not to make the same mistake this time. I kept my eyes on the track for the whole race. I don't think I even blinked, though it was so quick there was hardly time anyway.

The judge yelled, "Go!" and a wave of oily brown bodies hurtled down the track and crashed over the finish line. There were no collisions or fouls, and no one lagged too far behind or raced ahead.

The stadium erupted into passionate arguments about who had won, but the judge declared Dionysodoros of Taranto the winner, and his decision was final.

Dionysodoros attempted a victory lap, but he'd barely reached the far side of the track when his fans got down from the stands and mobbed him.

I was pleased for them, but I really think it's time Athens won something. At least I know for sure we'll have a victory by this time tomorrow.

GET REAL

Athletes at the Olympic Games were competing for wreaths made from the branches of a sacred olive tree, not for money. Or at least that was the idea. In truth, they would also become rich. Their city-states would often reward them with hundreds of drachmas on their return, as well as perks such as free food for life.

The Second Evening

I was worried Dracon might be too nervous to sleep, but once again, he nodded off right away. I struggled again, so I got up to wander around.

As the bright moon rose, I saw a huge crowd heading toward the sanctuary. I followed them and ended up at a small mound of earth. I asked a man with a gray beard what was going on, and he said they were honoring Pelops, the founder of the games, who's buried there.

A bleating black ram was brought onto the mound, and a priest muttered a prayer before slitting its neck. He then poured its blood into a pit in the ground.

I wandered back into the village, where lots of parties were breaking out. The winning cities were celebrating noisily, while the losing ones were discussing which tactical mistakes they'd made.

I ended up back at our tent, where I'm lying next to a snoring Dracon. Not long now until I get to find out what it feels like to celebrate an Olympic victory.

GET REAL

The ancient Greeks told a few different myths about the origin of the Olympic Games. One was that they began as chariot races held by King Pelops. Visitors to the games would honor him by sacrificing a black ram on the second night.

The Third Day of the Olympics

This is a disaster. Everything has gone wrong, and I don't know what to do.

I managed to get just a few hours of sleep last night before it was time to get up and fetch Dracon's bread and water. The sun was just coming up, and the food stalls were reasonably quiet for once. There were still some noisy people awake and partying, but most had either made it back to their tents or found a patch of ground to pass out on.

There was a different man from usual at the bread stall. He was thin, with a long nose, and I wondered if I recognized him from somewhere. But he gave me the bread for half an obol with no haggling, so I didn't really question it.

I went back to our shelter, where Dracon had woken up and was stretching his arms and legs to get ready. I went off to get his water, walking all the way to the mountain stream to avoid the filthy river.

106

When I returned, I found myself gasping and dropping the waterskin.

Dracon was lying on his back and groaning. He was flushing red, and there were chunks of half-chewed bread all around him. I ran over and smelled an unmistakable whiff of vomit.

Dracon was ill. He'd been preparing for this day for four years, and now that it had arrived, he was too sick to even move.

I raced back for the fallen waterskin and poured what was left into Dracon's mouth. He tried to swallow it but could only spew it back up again.

I told Dracon to get up and run it off, but he couldn't even stand, let alone throw or jump or wrestle.

Without knowing what else to do, I raced off to find one of the judges. I found a man with gray hair and purple robes eating his breakfast figs inside the council house. I told him what had happened, and he followed me back to our shelter.

I was hoping that Dracon would be back on his feet, and the judge would scorn me for making a big deal about nothing. But Dracon looked even worse. Now his face was pale, and he was trembling slightly.

The judge crouched down and examined Dracon. He confirmed Dracon was too ill to compete and told him to try again in another four years.

Four years? I told him Dracon was meant to win, and we should put off the entire pentathlon until he was better.

108

You'll have to do it. It's the will of the gods.

The judge said we were here to honor Zeus first and foremost, and it didn't matter if some missed out on their events. Fighters died, runners crashed, and pentathletes fell ill at the last moment. It was just the nature of sports.

Dracon pushed himself up with one trembling hand and grabbed my wrist with the other. He managed to force out a whisper before sinking back down again. And what he said sent my whole body into a panic.

He said that the gods had made him sick because they didn't want him to compete. They wanted me to compete instead.

The judge considered this for a moment. He said it was highly unusual, but if it was really what the gods wanted, he would allow it.

I tried to tell him he shouldn't allow it, as I was absolutely terrible at all the events, but it was like he couldn't hear me.

He strode back toward the sanctuary and beckoned me to follow.

There were three other judges inside the

council house, who were eating olives and bread dipped in wine. The judge with gray hair explained my situation to them, and they all agreed that I should take part if it was the will of the gods.

I tried again to explain how I didn't want to take part, because I'd be awful, but none of them listened.

Before I knew what was happening, I was repeating the sacred oaths and being marched to the stadium.

Soon afterward, I was lining up with the competitors for the first event, which was the sprint. All the others were much taller and stronger than me. They had intense looks of concentration on their faces, except for the Spartan, who kept glancing at me and chuckling to himself.

I tried to tell myself I had a chance to bring glory back to Athens. It wasn't much of a chance, but it was there. For example, all the other runners might bump into one another and fall over. Or they might get confused and run the wrong way.

And besides, I'd never even tried to sprint before. I might turn out to be a complete natural. The finishing line looked so close. Maybe if I pushed myself really hard, I could win it? The others all had longer strides, of course, so effectively they didn't have as far to run. But I was lighter, and with the right burst of speed, I could finish in no time.

One of the judges stood at the starting line and told us all to take our places. The others struck the regular pose, with their left feet forward with the toes on the front of the line and their arms stretched out.

112

I wondered if I should try something different, like sticking both my hands in the air or balancing both feet on the edge of the stone. After all, if everyone else was doing the same thing, I might chance upon a great new method no one had tried before. But I didn't have time to decide, so I just went with the same technique as the others.

The judge shouted, "Go!" and I told my body to run to the finish line. The sprint had gone by in a blink while I'd been watching, and I thought taking part would be the same.

That turned out to be wrong. It all went horribly slowly, and I was aware of my failure at every stage.

I felt my legs and arms shuffling along, and at first, I thought I was actually going to keep up. Then the others moved away, and there was nothing I could do to reach them. It seemed as though the faster I ran, the farther away they got.

I somehow managed to look around at the crowd as I was going. It was so weird seeing all their shouting faces. Most of them were gazing at the actual race, which was now going on a few feet ahead of me. A clump of confused people were looking at me, and I guessed they must have been the Athenians. They'd turned up to see Dracon bring glory to their city, and instead they were watching a young boy make them look like idiots.

The others swept over the line. From my position behind everyone, it looked like they all won. But unfortunately, the judge declared Ariston the winner.

Spartan fans rushed down to congratulate him, and some got to the finish line before I did. But at least the celebrations distracted most of the crowd from my pathetic performance.

Sadly, the same can't be said of the next event, which was the javelin. The whole crowd had to watch us take our turns individually, so everyone noticed me this time.

I went fifth, just after a man from Corinth who had made the crowd gasp with his performance. I made the crowd gasp too, but I think they were just shocked that I'd been allowed to take part at all.

Everyone had three attempts to get their best distance, which was annoying. I'd have preferred it if we'd only had one throw. Then the crowd might have thought I was usually brilliant but just had an unlucky try.

Whoosh!

At least the practice I'd had with Dracon meant I knew how to tie the leather strap around my fingers and fling the javelin. I'd have been disqualified right away if I'd just grabbed it and chucked it.

I ran up and made my throw. The good news is that it was much better than the one I'd done while Dracon was training. It didn't land on the head of a single one of the judges, and it didn't accidentally kill anyone and plunge Athens into war with a rival city.

The javelin went down the track in exactly the right direction. It just didn't go very far. It flew high into the air before dipping and landing a little farther down.

I definitely got it higher than everyone else did. If height rather than distance had been the aim, I'd have been the clear winner. But it wasn't, and the distance was terrible. I could hear confused murmurs from the crowd as I went over to fetch the javelin.

The next throw went a little farther, but it still wasn't close to the general standard. The judge who was meant to be marking out the distances had to shuffle down from the far end of the track to measure my attempts.

Unfortunately, my last effort was the worst of all, and the crowd began to yell insults. A man at the front said he'd thrown sticks for his dog that went farther. A Spartan yelled that Athenians must be even weaker than he thought if I was the one they'd chosen for the pentathlon event.

But the worst insult of all came from a huge cluster of Athenian spectators high above me. They told me to give up and stop shaming them, and to never set foot in their glorious city again for the rest of my life.

The discus was next. I tried not to think about my practice attempt, when I'd tripped over and the discus had rolled briefly along the track before coming to a stop.

The crowd cheered all the other competitors, but when it was my turn, they were totally silent. A few seemed to be blushing with embarrassment, but I told myself they were probably just hot because of the sun.

118

I stepped up to the starting line, and the judge with gray hair handed me a round bronze slab. He told me this was a special discus kept in a treasury inside the sanctuary. He said it was only ever used by competitors in the pentathlon and I should honor Zeus with my effort. I felt like saying that when Zeus witnessed my effort, he'd probably flood Olympia and demand that the games be canceled forever.

I balanced the discus in my right hand. It was so heavy that I almost collapsed before I could even throw it.

I was too ashamed to make a big show of warming up, so instead I just twisted my body in the way Dracon always did and then let go of the discus.

To my amazement, the discus didn't fly off

the wrong way or roll pathetically along the ground. It flew through the air and landed not too far from where the other judge was standing. I hadn't done as well as the others, but I hadn't totally shamed myself, and none of the crowd was shouting abuse.

Not only was this a personal record for me, but it was also the only Olympic event I'd ever done okay in. I threw my hands into the air and cheered.

Now the crowd started yelling. I'd done worse than all the others, and yet I'd still chosen to celebrate. This didn't fit in with the spirit of the Olympics, and I wished I hadn't done it.

The Athenians told me to raise my standards and stop embarrassing them, while the Spartans did a lot of sarcastic cheering.

My next two attempts fell short of the first. The reaction of the fans had destroyed my confidence, and I just wanted it to be over. Plus, the crowd was getting angry as rival fans teased the Athenians and the Athenians yelled back, so I thought it would be safer for everyone if I got it over with quickly.

The only thing that slightly cheered me up was that Ariston didn't win the event. He went first and did a really good throw. You could tell from his smug grin that he really thought he had won, but a gigantic man from Thebes threw the discus even farther right at the end.

Next up was the long jump. I had to remind myself not to celebrate just jumping in the right direction, even though that would sadly be a personal best.

One of the judges disappeared at the start of
the event, but I didn't think much of it until
he returned with some musicians. There was
a man with a lyre, a man with a drum, and a
man with some pipes. The judge explained that
the other judges were worried that a riot might
break out if I was as bad as usual, so they'd
decided to calm the crowd with music.

When it was my turn, I took my weights from the judges and went to the starting line. I did my three jumps as quickly as possible, running up, swinging my arms out, pushing the weights back, and landing.

I was quite pleased with my efforts again, but I made sure not to celebrate.

The judges' plan to distract the crowd seemed to work. I could still hear a few insults, but most people were looking at the musicians, who had been ordered to circle me as I performed my pathetic jumps.

Sadly, Ariston did the longest jump by far, which meant a victory in wrestling would make him the overall winner.

Dracon had drawn him in the first round, which meant that I had to go up against him instead.

On the plus side, this meant I could stop him. It was a tall order, but all I had to do was somehow get him to the ground three times to deny him pentathlon glory.

I tried to summon up all my strength. If I was so exhausted after beating Ariston that I was instantly killed by my next opponent, it wouldn't matter. At least I'd die knowing I'd denied Sparta victory.

When it was our turn, we covered ourselves in dust and walked up to each other. Ariston was towering over me and blocking my view of the sun. My head barely came up to his chest.

I thought about how strange it must have looked to the crowd to see a small boy squaring up to a man the size of an average temple. Surely there would be no honor for him in beating someone so small?

124

I got my answer when the herald shouted our names. Everyone cheered for Ariston, but when my name was announced, the whole crowd clapped and chanted, "Kill him!"

I supposed they meant it. The Spartans wanted Ariston to win. The Athenians wanted me dead for bringing shame to their city. And neutral spectators just wanted to see something they could tell their friends about back home.

The judge went through the rules and promised he would whack us with the rod if we broke them.

He said that competitors usually began by locking foreheads, but as this wouldn't be possible without a stool, we should just lock arms.

I reached up and grabbed Ariston's dusty arms. It felt like holding tree branches. He grasped my upper arms with his huge fingers, and I could feel myself trembling. I willed myself to stop feeling afraid and start feeling angry.

He leaned down so that his head was just above mine.

"What a shame your friend got sick," he whispered. "I was looking forward to beating him."

Then he chuckled and added, "Such terrible timing, eh?"

It was at that point that I finally realized that the Spartans had done something to Dracon. They were the reason he'd gotten ill and missed the event.

I felt my grip on Ariston's wide arms tighten. Now I didn't have to make myself angry. I was already feeling that way.

Something occurred to me that gave me hope. If Sparta had cheated at the games, it wasn't just me that would be angry. It was Zeus himself.

I looked past Ariston's huge face and into the sky.

"Excuse me, Zeus," I said. "These Spartans have been cheating during your games. If that makes you angry, give me a sign."

I looked around. There was a small cloud coming over the top of one of the mountains. I would have preferred a bolt of lightning, but it would have to do.

"Good sign," I said. "Now fill my body with the strength of a thousand men so I can get revenge on these villains!"

My arms still felt pretty much the same, but I'd never tried to get help from the gods before, so I didn't know exactly what it would feel like.

"That's a serious accusation you just made," whispered Ariston. "It's just as well you won't be around to share it with anyone."

The judge told us to start. I let go of Ariston's arms and hopped from side to side.

I decided that grabbing Ariston around the waist would be the best use of my new Zeus-given powers. I couldn't wait to hear the surprised gasps of the crowd as I slammed him to the ground.

I shoved my arms around his side and tried to summon my divine strength. Then something weird happened. I found that I was on the ground instead of him. I was gazing up at the blue sky and listening to the crowd chanting, "Kill him!"

The judge declared that Ariston was leading by a point and told us to get back into position.

"Okay, Zeus," I muttered, looking back up at the sky. "I know you're probably busy turning into a swan or something, but I could really use your help here. Please fill me with strength so I can defeat this crook."

The judge told us to start again. I tried grabbing Ariston by the shoulders this time. I was on my back and struggling for air again before I had time to take in what was going on.

Two points to Ariston.

We got back into position. The cries of "Kill him!" got louder and louder.

"I'd better give the people what they want," said Ariston. "Any last words?"

It was about then that I realized I must have called on Zeus at a bad time, and I needed to rethink my strategy.

I decided that the people couldn't dislike me any more than they already did, so I might as well adopt a tactic that was bound to be unpopular. I ran away.

The jeering from the crowd grew even louder, which I hadn't thought would be possible.

I kept glancing over my shoulder for Ariston, and every time he was about to catch up, I dodged and went a different way. I thought I might be able to keep this going until Ariston fell over three times, but I hadn't taken the judge into account. While I was concentrating on avoiding Ariston, he approached from the other side and thrashed me with his rod.

I recoiled from the painful stings and found myself flailing on the ground. The judge declared Ariston the winner, but neither he nor the crowd were pleased.

Ariston wanted to fight the last match again so he could kill me like the cowardly rat I was. The fans were on board with this, but the judge said we had to move on and his decision was final.

I think the frustration must have helped Ariston, because he unfortunately went on to win the whole contest, and therefore the whole pentathlon.

I got away from the stadium while the Spartans were swarming down to celebrate their victory. I didn't exactly want to hang around and meet the crowd after my disgraceful efforts.

Dracon was still lying down and looking green when I returned. He managed to ask what had happened in a quiet, croaky voice. I think he was expecting me to reveal I'd won a shocking victory. But I had to admit that the only shocking thing had been the standard of my performances.

I told him I thought the Spartans had cheated. He was so angry he tried to get up and find them, but he was too weak to even stand, let alone give them the thrashing they deserved, and he collapsed back to the ground.

He's sleeping again now, and I'm sitting next to him and deciding what to do. I can't go to the judges with my suspicions because I don't have any evidence, but I don't know how to get any either.

GET REAL

Music was a big feature of the ancient Olympics. Trumpeters got the attention of crowds, and then speakers called heralds addressed them. Eventually contests for the best trumpeters and heralds were added to the games. Other musical instruments, such as the flute and lyre, were sometimes used to accompany events like the long jump.

Chapter 6
—
A Wicked Plot

The Evening of the Third Day

I just read back over my writing to try and work out what the Spartans have been up to. It's helped me remember that a thin man with a long nose watched Dracon train one day. He sounds similar to the strange person who was in the food stall this morning.

Were they the same person? And if so, what does it mean?

The man with the long nose is a gambler, and he saw that I was Dracon's assistant. Could he have given me poisoned bread to make Dracon ill so he could bet on Ariston?

It all sounds possible. I'm off to investigate.

Slightly Later on the Evening of the Third Day

Okay, well, that didn't last long. I couldn't get anywhere near the food stalls, because angry people kept recognizing me from my performance earlier.

A man with a scar on his cheek said I was a disgrace to Athens and the only way I could make it up to him was if he sacrificed me to Zeus. I told him I was busy, but I'd think about it.

I ducked away but ran past a storyteller who pointed at me and shouted, "There's the coward from Athens!"

I had to weave in and out of an oncoming crush of people just to escape with my life.

I came back here to our shelter to rethink things. I found a razor and some honey in Dracon's bag, and I've managed to use them to create a cunning disguise. I cut all the hair off my head and stuck it to my chin with the honey. Genius!

I'd like to think it makes me look like a wise old man, though I suspect it actually makes me look like someone whose friends have played a cruel trick on him while he was sleeping.

It doesn't really matter. As long as no one recognizes me from my terrible pentathlon effort, I don't mind.

Much Later on the Third Day

I managed to make it to the bread stall without anyone realizing who I was. The usual scowling man was back in the stall, and I asked him who had been his mysterious morning assistant.

He said he doesn't have an assistant, and that his stall doesn't open until he wakes up just after sunrise.

That confirmed my suspicions but left me with nothing to follow. I couldn't think of anything to do except wander around the village and see if I bumped into the Spartans or the gambler. I thought they might be throwing a party somewhere, but there was no sign of them.

140

They're probably plotting some more dishonesty for tomorrow, and I'm running out of time to stop them.

As night fell, the musicians, scientists, and philosophers started to perform again, and people gathered around them. The poets were getting the biggest crowds of all, and I wandered up to see what they were saying.

It turned out they were all trying to outdo each other with their description of the small boy from Athens who had been the worst competitor in the history of the games.

As if what I'd done wasn't bad enough, they were all exaggerating to draw in more people. In one version, my performance in the long jump was so poor that it turned everyone in the audience to stone. In another, I accidentally threw the javelin directly upward, only for it to plummet back down and kill me, to huge cheers from the crowd.

I need to find some proof about the gambler and the Spartans so everyone can get angry with them instead.

Cheating is surely much worse than simply being bad at sports.

The Fourth Day

Dracon felt a little better today, and he offered to go and confront the dishonest Spartans. I told him to hold off until I had some evidence. Just going out and attacking them without proof would make us as bad as them.

Today's events were all horse racing ones in the hippodrome, which has an even bigger track than the stadium, and even bigger stands for spectators. I wandered around early this morning and found it was already full of men staking out their places.

A few groups were taking bets on the races, so I asked them if they'd seen the thin man with the long nose. Most of the ones who had were pretty angry with him. They said he'd taken lots of money from them thanks to Ariston's unexpected victory.

This backed up my idea that he was guilty, but it didn't help me track him down. I soon found a man who'd placed a bet with him the night before. He said the thin man was backing Charilaus of Sparta in the horseback race, but this was stupid because everyone knew Hieron of Syracuse would win.

I decided to go to the stables next.

I could see no signs of the Spartans or the gambler when I got in, so I went over to tell Aethon about my problems.

I started by revealing it was me behind the clever beard disguise, though I didn't feel like he was fooled by it anyway. I was just getting into my pentathlon failure when I heard some people enter and I stopped talking.

I glanced at the doorway and saw Ariston, Charilaus, the gambler, and another man with a red beard.

The cheats were right there, no doubt carrying out another foul plot.

I thought about confronting them, but I realized it would be too easy for them to get rid of me

144

while no one else was around. Instead, I threw
myself down on the ground to keep out of sight.

The man with the red beard kept watch at the
door while the others held back the head of one
of the horses and made it drink something
from a jug.

They moved on to another horse and did the
same. This time I got a waft and realized what
they were up to. They were making the horses
drink wine.

Sluurrp

So this is why the gambler was sure Charilaus would win. He's the only one whose horse will be able to run properly.

I kept myself pressed to the ground until they finished. When I was sure they were gone, I raced out of the stables and over to the council house. At last, I had evidence. I could tell the judges what I'd seen, they could come and examine the horses, and before long they'd be adding a new Olympic event of hitting the wicked Spartans with rods.

The crowds were growing thicker on the stand behind me. It wouldn't be long until the chariot race began, and everyone wanted a good spot for that.

There were only two judges inside the council house when I arrived: the one with gray hair

who'd checked on Dracon with me, and another
with wispy brown hair.

I didn't want to go through my story over
and over again, so I told them to gather all
the judges at once, as I had a very important
announcement to make.

They seemed annoyed, especially as I was
interrupting their breakfast figs, but I was very
insistent, and the man with gray hair went off
to fetch the rest.

Four other judges were herded in, and all
grumbled about being distracted from their
chariot race preparations.

The last judge was ambling in as I began my
story. I'd just told them all I had sensational
news to share, when I had to stop. I recognized

the final judge. This was the man with the red
beard who'd been keeping watch at the
stable door.

I stared at the judges with my mouth open.
There was no way I could go ahead with my
story. The man with the red beard would say I
was lying, and they'd have me flogged before we
could get anywhere near the stables. But I had
no idea what to say instead.

The judge with gray hair told me to hurry up,
as they all had important things to do.

I said the first lie that came into my head,
which was that I was a rider called Alexias
from Athens who had only just arrived due to
being attacked by bandits on the way. I said I'd
trained for the horseback race for four years
and didn't think I should be denied the chance
to compete because of some cowardly thieves.

As I was saying all this, I started to realize it wasn't actually a bad idea. I could run the race on Aethon, and reveal the truth afterward, with the drunken horses behind me for evidence. The judge with the red beard might still want me flogged, but perhaps some of the others would believe me.

The judges considered my plea. The one with the red beard kept wiping sweat from his forehead and saying it was too late to change things, but the others agreed that they should make an exception for someone who'd endured such bad luck.

I thanked them and ran straight back to the stables so I could guard Aethon until the race.

Aethon really seemed to be listening as I told him all about the event he'd be taking part in and what he had to do.

The stables were much fuller now. All around us were riders, trainers, and grooms who were preparing for the chariot race.

As the start drew nearer, they began to lead their horses out to the gates on the hippodrome track.

Dracon had said the chariot race was one of the most exciting parts of the games, and it was a shame to be stuck in the stables and missing it. But I knew the crooked judge would tell the Spartans about me, and they'd sneak in and feed Aethon wine if I left him alone.

Soon it was time for the race to begin. I had to make do with imagining the spectacle unfolding a few feet away. Each chariot, with four horses attached, would be guided into the starting gates while the rider took hold of the reins.

150

I could hear a trumpet, followed by a herald announcing the names. Then the gates opened, and hooves thundered along the track.

There was a thud, followed by screams and gasps as two of the chariots collided. I winced, and I think Aethon did too, if that's possible.

The yelling from the crowd got louder and louder until finally it turned into cheers. The race was over, and the winners were celebrating.

It sounded like I'd missed a good one, and I hoped I would get to watch a chariot race properly one day.

Soon after that, more people entered the stables. These were the owners and riders for the horseback race. While all the chariot riders had been tall and strong, the horseback racers were all small, thin boys.

Charilaus and his Spartan friends were there. They looked over at me and scowled, but I took no notice.

Burp

I grabbed Aethon's reins and led him out to the hippodrome. Some of the other riders were ordering their horses to snap out of it and walk straight. The wine had obviously kicked in.

There was a long line of wooden gates on the starting line, all controlled by a clever system of ropes that meant the riders on the longer outside track had a little more time. It was all very efficient, or at least it would have been if all the horses hadn't kept bashing into the sides and whinnying drunkenly.

Aethon and I were placed on one of the inside gates, right next to Charilaus. He was holding the reins in one hand and a leather whip in the other. I realized I was the only rider who didn't have a leather whip.

Charilaus glanced over at me and said there was no way I could win. He said he was the greatest rider in the world, and he wasn't going to let an idiot with a false beard steal victory from him. He added that he knew I was the Athenian imbecile from the pentathlon, and he expected me to do just as badly in this event.

I peered over the top of the wooden gate at the stone turning point in the distance. We just had to get around that and come back down the track to reach the finish line. It was such a short distance, I was sure Aethon would do well. But avoiding all the confused horses who'd drunk the wine was going to be difficult.

A trumpet blasted out, and the herald shouted our names. My false one got a huge cheer, so at least no one in the crowd had worked out I was the disgraced pentathlete.

The first gate opened, and the race was underway. Instead of bolting out, the horse cantered along, veering over to the wooden barrier at the edge of the track. There were confused murmurs from the crowd.

The next horse went faster but couldn't stop itself from staggering side to side.

154

Just as Charilaus's gate was about to open,
I told him I knew what he'd done, and I was
going to tell everyone when the race was over.

He didn't have time to taunt me back, so he just
scowled, gripping his whip so tightly that his
fingers went white.

He sped away, much quicker than the others.
Then Aethon and I were off too.

Charilaus leaned forward on his horse, cracking
his whip. Two riders had already fallen onto
the track ahead of us, thrown by their swaying
horses. Charilaus ordered his horse to trample
them, but it steered around them, earning itself
another lash.

Aethon followed just behind, keeping pace with
the Spartan horse.

Two of the horses ahead of us had stopped, while another had turned around and was running the wrong way. There were loud and angry cries from the fans.

The race really fell apart at the turning post. Some of the horses kept going straight, pummeling into the wooden barrier. A few others collided, creating a writhing mess of fallen horses and boys.

Charilaus weaved around the carnage, and Aethon followed. We made it through, along with two other confused horses, neither of whom had their riders.

Charilaus struck his whip in a mad blur, and his horse pelted forward. I was surprised to find Aethon running just as fast without any whipping. It was really tough to stay on at that speed, and I had to lean forward and grip the reins with all my strength.

Soon, we were right alongside Charilaus and heading for the finish line. He glanced over and hissed. He dashed his hand out, and it looked like he was still whipping his horse. But then I felt a painful sting on my arm and realized he was sneakily aiming at me.

I hoped one of the judges would see and disqualify him, but they were all too distracted by the chaos at the turning point.

Charilaus whipped me again, cutting a deep gash on my arm. I winced and flinched to the side, almost falling off. Aethon veered slightly away, and Charilaus missed me with his next strike.

The finishing line was just ahead. As Charilaus prepared to strike again, I noticed that one of the riderless horses was catching up on the other side. It was out of control and heading straight for him.

I just needed to keep him distracted until it could crash into his horse. I pretended to cry, taking my right hand away from the reins so I could rub the gash he'd cut on my arm.

He grinned and drew his whip back again. I begged him not to do it, yelling at him to show mercy.

This kept his attention just long enough. With the finish line in sight, the riderless horse careened right into his, and they both went down.

I still had my head twisted back to watch Charilaus flailing next to the fallen horses when a huge cheer went up.

Aethon and I had crossed the finish line. Somehow, I had become an Olympic champion.

Everything happened very fast after that. Athenian spectators rushed down to congratulate me as Aethon came to a halt. I got down and they crowded around, cheering and patting my back.

The judge with gray hair ran up and tied a red victory ribbon around my head. He asked where the owner of the horse was, and for a moment, I was too shocked to even remember who it was.

But then I saw Dracon hobbling down from the front of the stand. He still looked pretty green, but at least he was back on his feet again. I pointed to him, and the judge went over to congratulate him too.

I was so pleased with all the attention that I forgot about my plan to expose the cheating Spartans. When I remembered, I dashed over to the trumpeter and got him to silence the crowd.

160

I knew my voice wouldn't be loud enough, so I grabbed the herald and got him to repeat everything I said.

I revealed that the reason the other horses had done so badly was because the Spartans had made them drink wine. I said that a thin man with a long nose had been part of the plot so he could place dishonest bets on a Spartan victory. Hissing rang out around the crowded stands.

I said that Charilaus had known all about it too, but when I turned around to point him out, he'd gone.

There was no sign of Ariston or the gambler either. They'd all snuck away as soon as they knew they'd lost.

We did manage to catch one of the villains, though. I spotted the judge with the red beard trying to run away, and got the herald to tell everyone that he'd been part of the plot too.

He tried to dash away, which only proved his guilt.

Two of the other judges chased after him, grabbed his arms, and marched him back.

The judge with the red beard attempted to turn the attention back on me by revealing I was the same boy who'd lost the pentathlon, now wearing a false beard and going under a different name. He said I was hardly in a position to lecture anyone about honesty.

The judges crossed their arms and stared at me. Even the herald peered at me with suspicion.

I took a deep breath. I hadn't meant to go into

the whole thing in front of everyone, but the crooked judge had left me with no choice.

I rubbed away what was left of my beard and admitted I was the same boy. But then I got the herald to explain that I'd only had to take over in the pentathlon at the last minute because the Spartans had poisoned Dracon's bread.

The judge with the red beard said he had known nothing about that particular plan and would never have helped the Spartans with it. He might have been telling the truth, but it was too late. He'd brought the sacred duties of the judges into disrepute, and they were going to have to punish him. They all gathered around him and beat him with their rods.

As Dracon and I walked out of the hippodrome, lots of men offered to try and find the gambler and the cheating Spartans for us. But now the sun is starting to set, and no one has managed yet.

I expect they fled the site as soon as I started telling everyone about their crimes. But whether it was by sea or land, no one seems to know.

Dracon says the gods will punish them soon enough, so we should leave it to them. Ariston may have won the pentathlon, but now he'll never have the glory that goes with victory. He'll be remembered as a cheat forever.

Chapter 7

Olympic Champion

The Evening of the Fourth Day

Lots of men offered to buy me food and drink as I walked around the village tonight, and pretty much everyone promised to kill the cheating Spartans if they ever saw them.

Even men from Sparta itself felt the same. A man with curly black hair said that Ariston, Charilaus, and the others had brought shame on his great city, and they would be slaughtered if they ever set foot in it again.

So it looks as though they'll get their punishment even if the gods don't deal with them. They'll never be able to return home, and they'll have to survive as best as they can by traveling from town to town and keeping their true identities secret.

The poets had big crowds again, and thankfully they'd moved on from their odes about my terrible performance in the pentathlon. They were all inventing stories about the villainous Spartans, which claimed that they did things like trip people up in the sprint and bludgeon them with their discuses.

One of the poets spotted me and came up with a victory ode about my heroic performance in the horseback race. After he'd finished, he asked me what I thought about it. I said I'd liked it, but I thought Aethon should have gotten more of a mention. After all, he was the one who'd run the race. All I did was cling to him.

The poet then composed a wonderful ode to the swift white steed the gods had gifted to a small boy from Athens. I tried to remember it so I could recite it to Aethon on the way home.

The Fifth Day of the Olympics

There were no more contests today, as it was time for the closing ceremony. I had to join a procession of all the winners through the sanctuary to the Temple of Zeus, where we

were given crowns of leaves cut from the sacred
tree. As the owner of Aethon, Dracon got to
wear the crown for the horseback race, but I'm
happy with my ribbon.

After that, everyone went off to celebrate
again. I must have told my story about beating
Charilaus a hundred times, but there were
always more people who wanted to hear it.
It seems that being a winner is even more
exhausting than competing.

GET REAL

*The final day of the Olympics was reserved
for the closing ceremony, where winners
would march through the sanctuary and
receive their victory crowns as well as
fruit and leaves. These were symbols of the
good harvest with which the gods would
hopefully reward everyone.*

The First Day After the Olympics

We were setting off for home again this morning, with me on Aethon and Dracon following behind, when a huge group of men on horses raced to catch up. They said they were going back to Athens too, and no champion should have to go on foot. One of them pulled Dracon up onto his horse, and we continued along much faster.

The only problem was that they wanted to hear my victory story over and over again. I had been looking forward to giving it a rest after the last two days.

The Third Day After the Olympics

We're making good progress, and it's been a very comfortable journey so far. The men have insisted on giving us their food and fetching us water. They've even built our shelter at night.

Last night, two of them rode ahead instead of staying behind to sleep, so they must have been in a hurry. We should be back in Athens very soon. I can't wait to see Dad's face when he spots the ribbon on my head. He won't believe I actually won one of the events. He'd probably think I was lying if I didn't have Dracon to back it up.

The Fifth Day After the Olympics

We arrived in Athens this morning and soon discovered the reason the other men had gone on ahead. They'd already told everyone about my victory.

The whole route from the walls of the city to my parents' house was lined with cheering fans. They were congratulating me on winning the race and beating the Spartans. People kept leaping forward to touch me, Dracon, and Aethon, just so they could say that they'd been close to Olympic champions.

So much for giving my victory story a rest. Judging by the size of the crowd, I'll be retelling it for the rest of my life.

As we climbed the hill to my parents' house, I could see Dad, Mom, and all of our slaves waiting outside.

I got down from Aethon and led everyone into our courtyard. I felt like one of the old war heroes addressing the crowds in Olympia as I stood on my stool and went through every part of my story over and over again.

Well, perhaps not every part. I skipped over my terrible performances in the pentathlon, leaving it vague except for the bits about the Spartans' cheating.

174

But I made up for it by describing the horseback race in so much detail that it took ten times as long as the race itself.

Dad said he was very proud of me, and I couldn't stop myself from blushing.

Then he said something I hadn't really thought about. He reminded me that the oracle had told him I'd win a great victory in the field of battle and be cheered by huge crowds. And now the prophecy has come true. Only it wasn't a battle in a war she'd been talking about, but a sporting battle.

It just goes to show you should listen to oracles, however unlikely their predictions might sound. I always wanted to be a hero, and now I am one.

And I managed to do it without getting stabbed by an enemy's spear or sword. The worst I had to suffer was a lash on the arm from a pathetic Spartan boy.

Games are pretty amazing, really. I've decided I prefer them to war.

The End

The Ancient Olympics

Athletic competitions were incredibly popular in ancient Greece, and people would travel from miles around to visit them, with some coming from as far as modern-day Spain and Egypt.

The four major events were the Olympic, Pythian, Nemean, and Isthmian Games. The most famous were the Olympic Games. These were held at a sacred site known as Olympia, to the southeast of Elis. It was quite far from major cities like Athens and Thebes, and most visitors would spend a long time getting there.

Those who braved the epic journey by sea or land could watch events such as the sprint, the pentathlon, and the chariot race. They could also enjoy other forms of entertainment, such as music and poetry, and even catch up on the latest ideas from scientists and philosophers. They would celebrate late into the night and perhaps even attend a lavish banquet held in honor of one of the winners.

As well as sport and fringe events, they'd witness religious ceremonies. The games were held to honor Zeus, and they included ceremonies like holy processions and animal sacrifices.

The ancient Olympics ran for over a thousand years, until they were banned by the Romans in 394 CE. But the tradition was revived in 1896, when the first modern Olympic Games were held in Athens.

How Do We Know About Ancient Greece?

Alexander's diary takes place well over two thousand years ago. So how do we know so much about such a distant time?

One reason is that some written records have survived. In many cases, the original Greek documents have been lost, but later copies made by Romans have survived.

Another great source of information is pottery. The Greeks decorated their pots with detailed scenes from everyday life. In the case of the Olympics, we can spot things like the leather thongs wrapped around the hands of boxers and the shape of the weights used for the long jump.

Archaeologists have uncovered many important Greek towns and cities, as well as discovered the wrecks of ancient ships in the ocean. The site of Olympia was discovered in the late eighteenth century and has been gradually excavated. It is now a popular tourist attraction.

Timeline

776 BCE

This is the date of the first games, according to a list written much later. Some people estimate the real date to have been around 700 BCE. At first, the Olympics were a small local festival featuring athletes from nearby places such as Elis.

Timeline

500 BCE

The "archaic period" of Greek history
ends and the "classical period" begins.
This is a golden age of culture, producing
many great poets, philosophers, and
scientists. By this time, the Olympics have
developed into a major festival, attracting
competitors from all over the Greek world.

490 BCE

The Greek solider Pheidippides is said
to have run all the way from Marathon
to Athens to deliver news of a military
victory. This inspired the "marathon"
long-distance race, though it didn't become
part of the Olympics until the modern era.

Timeline

323 BCE

The death of Alexander the Great signals the end of the "classical period" and the beginning of the "Hellenistic period" of Greek history.

146 BCE

Greece falls under Roman rule following the Achaean War. The games continue and are now open to all citizens of the Roman Empire.

394 CE

The Roman emperor Theodosius I bans all pagan festivals, including the Olympic Games.

1766

The ancient site of Olympia is discovered by the English traveler Richard Chandler.

Timeline

1796

An "Olympic Festival" is held in
Revolutionary France.

1875

A major excavation at the site of Olympia,
carried out by a team of German
archaeologists, begins.

1892

Baron Pierre de Coubertin creates the
International Olympic Committee (IOC).

1896

The first modern Olympic Games are held
in Athens.

Timeline

1908
The Olympic Games are held in London for the first time.

1916
The Olympic Games are canceled because of the outbreak of World War I.

1920
The Antwerp Olympics sees the first appearance of the Olympic flag and the Olympic Oath.

1924
The first Winter Olympics are held at Chamonix in France.

*T*imeline

1928

The Olympics in Amsterdam see the first
appearance of the Olympic torch.

1936

The Olympic Games are held in Berlin,
Germany, where Adolf Hitler tries to use
them for propaganda purposes.

1940 and *1944*

The Olympic Games are canceled twice
because of World War II.

1948

A forerunner of the Paralympic Games is
held at Stoke Mandeville in England.

Timeline

1956

The first boycotts for political reasons
take place during the Olympic Games in
Melbourne, Australia.

1960

The first official Paralympic Games are held
in Rome, Italy.

1964

South Africa is banned (until 1992) from
taking part in the Olympics because of its
apartheid policy.

1988

At the Seoul, Korea, Olympics, professionals
are allowed to compete for the first time.

Timeline

2012

London becomes the first city to host the
Olympic Games three times.

2020

The Olympic Games are postponed due to the
global coronavirus pandemic.

Ancient Olympics Hall of Fame

Arrhichion of Phigalia

Arrhichion was a wrestler from the sixth century BCE who died while defending his pankration title. He managed to break his opponent's ankle while he was being strangled. His opponent gave in, but Arrhichion died of his injuries. Arrhichion was declared the winner and was remembered as someone who heroically chose death over surrender.

Chionis of Sparta

Chionis was an athlete who competed in the seventh century BCE. He is listed as winning the short sprint three times in a row and was also a champion at the long jump. His record jump of more than 23 feet (7 m) would still have been good enough to win at the first modern Olympic Games more than 2,500 years later.

Ancient Olympics Hall of Fame

Coroebus of Elis

The first-ever Olympic champion, Coroebus won the sprint in 776 BCE. Or at least he did according to a list written by Hippias, also from Elis, many years later. Could Hippias have been favoring local athletes? Maybe, but Elis is very close to Olympia, and we know the games started as a local festival, so let's give Coroebus the benefit of the doubt and include him in the hall of fame.

Glaucus of Carystus

It was said that this farm laborer from the sixth century BCE could hammer plows back into shape using just his fists. Spotting this, Glaucus's father entered him into the Olympic boxing event. As he was about to surrender in the final bout, his father shouted out to remind him of his plows, and he delivered a mighty winning punch.

Ancient Olympics Hall of Fame

Kyniska of Sparta

The Olympic Games were only for men, so
how did a woman from Sparta in the fourth
century BCE manage to win? Kyniska did it
by owning and training the horses that won
the chariot races in 396 BCE and 392 BCE.
A bronze statue of her chariot and horses
was placed in the sanctuary. The inscription
read: "I declare myself the only woman in all
Greece to have won this crown."

Leonidas of Rhodes

A runner from the second century BCE,
Leonidas achieved an amazing twelve
victories across four separate Olympic
Games. He had very impressive versatility,
winning at both the short sprint and the
race in armor, events which were commonly
thought to suit different types of athletes.

Ancient Olympics Hall of Fame

Milo of Croton

A wrestling superstar from the sixth century BCE, Milo won the Olympic title six times in a row. He was also a great military hero, leading the Crotoniates to victory over the Sybarites, apparently while wearing his Olympic crowns. His legendary feats of strength include carrying a bull on his shoulders and lugging his own bronze statue into place in Olympia.

Polydamas of Skotoussa

Polydamas was a pankration fighter from the fifth century BCE. As with many ancient Olympians, there are plenty of stories about his amazing strength. It was said he killed a lion with his bare hands, and could stop a speeding chariot by grabbing it as it went past. He's said to have died in a collapsing cave when he tried to hold the roof up.

Ancient Olympics Hall of Fame

Theagenes of Thasos

Theagenes was a versatile athlete who competed in the fifth century BCE, winning at boxing, pankration, and long-distance running. But the most famous story about him takes place after he died. It's claimed that an old enemy tried to attack a bronze statue of Theagenes, but it fell over and crushed him to death.

Modern Olympics Hall of Fame

Muhammad Ali

Muhammad Ali is the most famous boxer of all time. He won the light heavyweight championship in Rome in 1960 fighting under his birth name of Cassius Clay. Four years later (having turned professional), he won the world heavyweight championship by defeating the seemingly unbeatable Sonny Liston.

Three years later, he converted to Islam and changed his name to Muhammad Ali. In 1996, he was chosen to light the Olympic flame at the Atlanta Games.

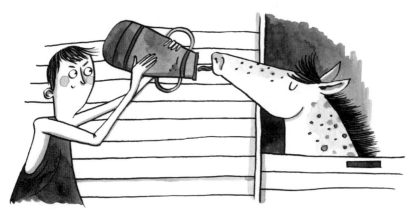

Modern Olympics Hall of Fame

Seb Coe

A British runner, Seb Coe had some wonderful tussles during the 1980s with his fellow countrymen Steve Ovett and Steve Cram. For precisely one hour in 1980 (until Ovett set a new time for the mile), he held all four of the classic middle-distance world records—the 800 meter, 1,000 meter, 1,500 meter, and the mile. Nobody had done that before, and nobody has repeated the achievement since.

Later in life, Coe led London's bid to stage the 2012 Olympics in the city and became chairman of the organizing committee.

Glossary

Archaeologist
Someone who studies history by examining objects from the past.

Archaic Age
The period in Greek history from around 800 BCE to 500 BCE.

Athena
The goddess associated with wisdom, practical skills, and warfare in Greek mythology.

Barbarian
The Greek word for a foreigner who spoke a different language.

City-State
An independent state formed of a city and the countryside surrounding it. The Greek term for it was "polis," which is where the word *politics* comes from.

Classical Age
The period in Greek history beginning around 500 BCE, a golden era for both culture and military strength.

Cyclops
A giant one-eyed monster from Greek mythology.

Drachma
An ancient Greek coin, made from silver.

Glossary

Haltares
A pair of stone or metal weights that were used to make athletes go farther in the long jump.

Hellenistic Age
The period following the death of Alexander the Great in 323 BCE, when Greek culture dominated his former empire.

Herald
Someone with a loud, clear voice who would make announcements to a crowd.

Heracles
A popular hero in Greek mythology, known as Hercules by the Romans.

Hippodrome
A track used for staging chariot and horse races.

Glossary

Ode
A poem addressing a particular person or object, often sung and accompanied by a musical instrument.

Odysseus
The legendary king of Ithaca and hero of the epic poem *The Odyssey*.

Lyre
A string instrument that looked like a small harp.

Nymph
A spirit of nature who takes the form of a beautiful young woman in Greek mythology.

Obol
An ancient Greek coin worth one-sixth of a drachma.

Oracle
A priest or priestess who can communicate with a god. Also the term for the message itself and the sacred place where it was given.

Glossary

Pankration
A violent wrestling contest in which everything was allowed except biting and eye-gouging.

Philosopher
Someone who tries to explain how things work and how society should be run.

Sacrifice
Killing a person or animal as an offering to the gods.

Sanctuary
An area of Olympia surrounded by a low wall which was filled with temples, shrines, and altars.

Siren
A creature from Greek mythology who lures sailors to their deaths with beautiful singing.

Trojan War
A legendary conflict in the city of Troy that featured in famous stories such as Homer's *The Iliad*.

Truce
An agreement between enemies to stop fighting for a certain time.

Zeus
The king of the gods in Greek mythology.

Discover More
LONG-LOST
SECRET DIARIES
and Laugh Along with
Our Hapless Heroes

by *Tim Collins*
illustrated by *Sarah Horne* and *Isobel Lundie*

AVAILABLE NOW

JOLLY
FiSH
PRESS